SHE DARED TO DREAM

JEEVIKA THAKUR

Made with ♥ on the Notion Press Platform
www.notionpress.com

For Juhi, Jaidev

without them I am nothing.

For Mumma and Pappa who give me strength.

For my closest friends Jeeshitha and Sahasra

who accept me as I am.

Contents

Foreword

Life doesn't come with a rulebook—just choices, consequences, and a whole lot of unexpected twists. This story dives into all of that.

It's about ambition, about struggle, about med school—but not just the grades and exams. It's about people, trust, and what happens when reality doesn't match the dream. It's raw, it's real, and it doesn't hold back.

But I won't spoil anything.

Just know—this story isn't here to tell you what to think. It's here to make you feel.

So settle in. It all starts now.

Preface

Aisha dreams big—bigger than the sky, bigger than the stars. She does not believe in limits. Every day, she imagines a new adventure, a new goal, and a new challenge to overcome.

This book is about her journey. It is about how she refuses to give up, how she keeps moving forward even when things are difficult. Aisha is not just a dreamer; she is a doer. She turns her dreams into plans, and her plans into reality.

There are moments of happiness and moments of struggle. But through everything, she learns one important lesson—dreams are only impossible if we stop believing in them.

Come, step into Aisha's world. A world where anything is possible if you have the courage to chase it.

Acknowledgements

Okay, wow—writing this book was a ride. Late nights, endless rewrites, and plenty of "do I even know what I'm doing?" moments. But I wasn't in it alone.

To my family—y'all are the best. Thanks for hyping me up and keeping me sane. To my friends and mentors, you always came through with advice, support, and just the right vibes when I needed them.

To my readers—you're the real MVPs. Seriously, this wouldn't mean anything without you.

And to everyone who helped out, whether you knew it or not—you made a difference, and I appreciate you.

Thanks for being part of this journey. You rock.

Prologue

I sit on a chair outside the doctor's office, psychiatrist to be precise waiting. The smell of disinfectant liquids mixing with the scent of coffee wafting from a vending machine nearby. The plaque on the door in front of me reads: Dr. Nagma Kapoor psychiatrist, the simple black letters feel heavier than they should. I've read them over hundred times patient's shuffle in and out. The door opens with a soft click, and a middle-aged man steps out, smiling at me as he passes. The receptionist calls my name, for a moment I hesitate my body get freezes my throat tightens.

"Ms. Aisha?", she says again I rise to my feet slowly, each movement feeling heavy my legs feel unsteady but somehow, I take a step then another. I think of all times I told myself I didn't need this, that I could handle it on my own but here I am walking toward something I don't fully understand. When I finally reach the doorway, I pause staring at the nameplate once more - Dr. Nagma Kapoor, psychiatrist.

"Come in", a soft voice call from inside which was warm yet professional, I push the door and step inside Dr. Kapoor sits behind a desk, she gestures toward a chair across from her. saying "Aisha please have a seat."

Slowly I sit on the chair, for a moment we sit in silence her eyes scanning me gently like she is searching for the words I can't yet say. "you've taken a big step by coming here why don't we start by talking about what brought you here?" my mouth feels dry and finally I look up, "I don't even know where to begin", I say.

"That's okay! Why don't you tell me your story, Aisha? start wherever you feel comfortable."

I take a deep breath and start to answer.

CHAPTER ONE

CHILDHOOD DESIRES

The dreams, aspirations and interests we naturally gravitate toward as children, many children fantasize about becoming astronauts, doctors, teachers or superheroes. These desires often come from characters they see in stories and movies. As we grow older, most of us tend to lose sight of our childhood dreams and settle for a more practical future. When I was in my second grade, my teacher asked us a question that seemed simple: "what do you want to be when you grow up?" the classroom filled with excited responses – doctors, engineers, astronauts and teachers. Everyone seemed to have a clear picture of their future, but when it was my turn, I froze. I didn't know what I wanted to be.

Hesitantly, I whispered "I don't know."

The room fell silent for a moment.

My teacher gave me a warm smile and said, "that's okay dear, you will figure it out someday."

Her words felt like a shield protecting me from embarrassment of not having an answer. It taught me that it was okay to be uncertain, that life is a journey where our dreams could evolve over time.For a long time, I didn't think much about future because I was a child who lived in the moment, and I was someone who wouldn't worry much about future because I thought I am gods Favorite, he wouldn't let anything bad happen with me.

By the time I reached middle school I began to dream bigger I found myself drawn to the world of fashion designing I imagined a future filled with creativity, sketching, designing and bringing vibrant ideas to life. It felt magical and exciting like a world where I could express myself,

but as time passed my dreams started to shift, I was not sure what to do when I grow up. I was so confused so I tried asking my mom. She told me, "It is okay to not know what to be when you grow up, you will figure it out one day, all you do now is participate in literally everything which will help you find your passion."

My mom's words pulled me out of uncertainty that had been weighing me down. I had spent so much time worrying, feeling like I was falling behind while everyone else seemed to have their future planned. But in that moment, I realized life isn't about rushing to find a path, every opportunity every challenge every experience was shaping me in ways I couldn't understand. Maybe I would find my passion in a classroom discussion or maybe unexpectedly in a hobby I never thought I'd enjoy. Perhaps it would come slowly and that was okay because life isn't a race to the finish it is a process a collection of moments that would guide me toward my purpose when the time was right. so instead of being consumed by worry, I choose to embrace the unknown to dive into everything with an open-heart trusting that someday I would finally understand what I am meant to do.

CHAPTER TWO

HIGH SCHOOL

School life, especially high school, is more than just grades and exams, it's full of emotions, friendships, heartbreaks, fights, pranks, and memories that stay with us long after we graduate. Friendships in school feel different. They start off simple like sitting next to someone in class but overtime they evolve into something deeper. These friendships are built on secrets, jokes, late-night study calls and promises that "we will always stay in touch no matter what."

I had my group – our little circle of chaos. We had everything: the studious one, the artist, the comedian, the overthinker, the topper and me, the chaotic one who is somehow always in trouble.

The bond we shared wasn't perfect as we had fights, misunderstandings, and the moments of losing touch but no matter what happened we always found our way back. That's the beauty of school friendships they stick even when life pulls us in directions. Let's talk about the mischievous side of school "the pranks" what is school life without pranks and troubles? One of our greatest achievements was we once convinced half the students that school would close early due to "An unexpected rain." And there were fights, silly arguments over stolen stationary and the dramatic "I am never talking to you again" moments that lasted exactly 2 hours. These little fights made school life fun. Of course, there were bigger fights too. The kind that came with misunderstandings, betrayal, or jealousy. But school teaches you things – that people make mistakes, that forgiveness is sometimes necessary and that friendships-real friendships can survive almost anything.

If you've ever had a school crush, you know exactly how it feels- the way air shifts when they walk into the room the way your heartbeat speeds up for absolutely no reason and the way your friends suddenly become expert studying every single interaction like it's the biggest moment of life. And yes, I'll admit it I had a light crush on a senior once. Nothing serious it wasn't love; it just made school life just a little bit more exciting. I remember the first time I noticed him was at a normal school event a casual competition where students gathered in the auditorium cheering for their classmates. I was sitting with my group laughing at whatever nonsense my friends were saying and then I noticed him for the first time, he was talking to a friend, laughing at something but not that kind of loud laugh people fake to fit in. It was real, effortless and genuine and for some reason something about it made me pause for a second longer than usual. From that day forward he was my crush. And if you've ever had crush, you know how ridiculous your brain gets.

Every interaction feels important like that one time he passed by me in the corridor, then there was the time we ended up standing next to each other. He didn't say a word I didn't say a word, but it felt like something. And of course, my wonderful friends made this even worse. Every time he walked into the room the teasing would begin, they would say, "Aisha, there he is! Go talk to him! "He totally saw you just now, you should at least say hi what if you secretly end up together? Imagine that" it wasn't that I was too shy to talk to him, I could have. But the truth is I didn't want to because this wasn't about turning a crush into something real. It was just about enjoying the quiet admiration, the fun of liking someone from a distance, the harmless excitement that made school life more interesting.

Eventually, he graduated. He left the school forever and just like that my little crush faded into nothing more than a memory. I never told him. I never tried to turn into something more and never regretted that. Because sometimes, a crush isn't meant to be anything more than what it is- a tiny spark in your everyday routine and honestly that was more than enough.

There is also this thing school teaches you, it's that teachers come in all varieties. Theres the strict one, the kind one, the funny one, the one who manages to make history lessons sound like an action movie, the chill one, and the inspiring one who makes you believe in yourself when you don't.

I had incredible teachers- the ones who pushed me, the ones who understood when I was struggling, the ones who made learning fun and even the ones who terrified me. And while we often complain about teachers the truth is they play a huge role in shaping us. The best ones teach us more than subjects: they teach us about life.

And how can I not talk about exams? Every student knows the feeling- sitting in the exam hall staring at a question in the exam

paper that looks like it's written in an alien language. Exams bring a different kind of chaos, the last-minute preparation, the whispered answers between friends, and there's panic, there's regret ("why didn't I study earlier!?"), and that desperate hope that somehow, miraculously we'll survive. But exams also teach us how to handle pressure, how to manage time and how to bounce back even after failure and let's be honest nothing feels better walking out of exam hall knowing its finally over.

School life is not perfect. Its messy, frustrating, exhausting, and sometimes even heartbreaking but it's also beautiful it's the place where we learn, laugh, fail, succeed, breakdown, stand up, Love, lose and grow. The friendships we form, the lessons we learn, the silly crushes we have, the pranks we pull, the teachers who shapes us, and how can I not talk about election fun? I will talk about it too, all of it stays with us forever.

And when we look back, we don't remember the stress of exams, the fear of failure, all we remember is laughter, the fun, the chaos and the moment that made school life one of the greatest chapters in our lives.

Because in the end, school isn't just a place – it's an experience.

CHAPTER THREE

ELECTION SELECTION

By the time I reached high school, I wasn't just another student; I was a proud part of student council. My journey in student council began in eighth standard. Back then, I wasn't the most popular student but that didn't stop me from participating in the elections, I wanted to get into the world of student leadership and wanted to get out of my comfort zone, so I started reaching out classmates, making conversations, and learning about their concerns. Slowly I built connections not just with my classmates but also with my juniors and seniors, I wasn't just asking for votes I was earning trust. Then came the election day everybody, casted there votes and when the results were announced, I had won! the moment was surreal- after weeks of hard work I had earned a seat at the table.

Becoming a student council member wasn't just an achievement it was a responsibility. My role allowed me to represent my school and to be a part of something bigger. As months passed, I found me growing- not just as a leader but as a person. I learned the art of decision making, and the power of teamwork.

When the time for elections arrived in my ninth grade, there was sense of anticipation and I had grown into someone who truly understood the weight and importance of student leadership, I participated again and there came the moment I would never forget- I was honored to be chosen as "HEAD GIRL".

Being Head Girl was more than just a title- it was a responsibility, and it meant standing at the forefront of my school, representing my peers. I embraced the challenges, knowing that leadership required courage and dedication. From organizing events to every task, I undertook helped me grow. I learned the power of teamwork, the importance of listening and the art of making decisions.

But beyond the responsibilities, being head girl was an adventure- one filled endless memories that I will cherish forever.

CHAPTER FOUR

AN UNEXPECTED FRIENSHIP

What truly made my time as head girl was sharing it with "Ryaan Mehra" the head boy, he was new, unfamiliar, and yet, somehow, he had won the title of head boy. I had worked hard to earn my position, dedicating years to student council, proving my leadership skills and building trust among my peers. Ryaan, on the other hand, had arrived out of nowhere and won everyone in a matter of weeks. It was rare for a newcomer to be chosen but Ryaan had something about him- an effortless charm, a quiet confidence.

At first, I didn't know much about him, he was different from other student leaders- calm, observant, and always carrying a hint of mystery. But as days passed, I realized that Ryaan wasn't just another student he was someone who could change my life forever.

Leading the school wasn't easy, between organizing events, handling students, and balancing academics, Ryaan and I barely had time to breathe but somehow, we made it work- side by side, figuring things out together.

At first our conversations were strictly professional. We discussed school policies, planned assemblies and coordinated student activities. But soon those discussions turned into something more- late night phone calls where we talked about everything and nothing at the same time.

"You think we'll survive this year?" I had joked one night,

exhausted from planning the annual school festival.

"Barely, but if we go down, we go down together," said Ryaan.

That was the thing about him- he never let anyone feel alone. Some nights, we would talk for hours sharing stories about our childhood's dreams and our fears.

"It's strange, I've never really had a place that felt like home. But this school.... it's different." He had said once.

I understood what he meant. There was something about our school, about the people, about the way we had found each other, that felt permanent.

Our bond grew stronger with each passing day, transforming from a friendly partnership into a deep and unbreakable friendship. Ryaan wasn't just my friend; He became my best friend. We shared countless laughs supported each other through tough times and made memories that I will cherish forever.

CHAPTER FIVE

THE BOARDS AND THE LAST SCHOOL MEMORIES

Class tenth- the year that felt like both a race and milestone. The board exams were approaching fast, and pressure was so much. Every conversation seemed to start with "did you study this chapter?" everyone was busy preparing, yet we all knew one thing- we were about to say goodbye to school life.

Despite the stress, there were moments of laughter. We promised each other that no matter what happened, we would meet again. A reunion was planned.

After writing our exams and weeks of waiting, the results were finally announced and every single one of us had passed with great marks, it felt like sleepless nights had finally paid off. With the results, our reunion became a reality.

When the day arrived, it felt strange seeing everyone in casual clothes instead of uniforms. We clicked pictures, laughed and talked about the memories we made in school.

Deep down, we all knew this was probably the last time we would all be together like this, so we soaked in every second- cherishing the conversation and endless laughter.

As the day came to an end, we talked about the paths we were about to take. I knew I would choose PCB (Physics, Chemistry, Biology) because science fascinated me, and I wanted to be doctor. My best friend, Ryaan Mehra decided on PCM as those were Ryaan's favorite subjects, I remember he was the one who always helped me with my math homework, and he would never get bored or irritated when I would ask him to solve all the problems that were given as homework. Others thought of picking commerce, humanities etc.,

As the sun began to set, we hugged, promising to stay in touch knowing that it would be difficult. But one thing certain, the memories we created we created in school would stay with us forever.

Walking back home, I felt a mix of emotions- Nostalgia, Excitement and Sadness because school life was over, but something told me the best was yet to come.

CHAPTER SIX

THE STRANGER IN THE RAIN

The summer after passing my 10th standard felt like a blank canvas- waiting to be painted with adventure, discovery and perhaps something unexpected.

I wanted to spend my time nicely, so I started filling the long days with books coffee and quiet escapes from the world.

That's how I found myself walking into a cafe on a rainy afternoon, the scent of freshly brewed coffee wrapping around me like a warm embrace, the city outside was alive with the rhythm of raindrops, the hum of conversations, the distant sound of car horns, but inside it was different- calm, and intimate.

I stepped toward a quiet corner, seeking warmth and then- I saw him.

Across the room, seated by the window was a man who seemed strangely familiar. His skin was dark and smooth, a mole rested on is lips that made him more striking, and his eyes were hazel in color his hair and eyebrows were thick, in chest brown shade, he was beautiful in a way that felt unsettling, like something out of a forgotten memory.

Our eyes meet, a second stretching into eternity. Then he took his drink and disappeared.

Days kept passing and I tried to forget him.

I filled my time with new hobbies- reading, writing, wandering through the citylike a poet searching for inspiration. I told myself it was just a moment, a stranger in a cafe, nothing more but something was different.

The way the rain had framed him like a scene from a novel. The way his gaze had held mine as if he knew something I didn't, and then- fate struck again.

It was those rare mornings where the sun and moon shared the sky, painting the world in soft gold and silver. I found myself at a crowed bookstore event, reaching the last copy of a popular romance novel- only to feel another hand on it, I looked up and there he was, the cafe stranger the one who vanished like as dream. For a second we were silent the world around us blurred. Then- (a playful argument)

"I saw it first", I said.

"Pretty sure I touched it first, but it is okay, you can take it.", he said with a deep and smooth voice which was like a slow pour of honey in warm tea- rich, steady and unshaken.

I thanked him and then we visited a cafe.

At the cafe I uttered without thinking- "oh gosh, you are too handsome" I froze for a second

"Had I said that out loud?"

he gave me a wide grin "yeah", he said leaning back.

I felt shy and wanted to disappear in my coffee cup but then, he left but not before slipping something inside my book cover-

A handwritten note and a number.

What happens next?

The book sat in my lap, its weight felt heavier than it should have been, but it wasn't the book that made my pulse race- it was the note tucked inside its cover.

I hesitated before opening it, my fingers trembling slightly as I unfolded the paper. The handwriting was beautiful with smooth strokes.

"Hey Aisha, it was nice seeing you at the cafe a few days back"

I froze I hadn't told him my name, how did he know?

"I know you cannot understand anything, that's why I am giving you my number, call me whenever you feel like calling." The words felt heavy, charged with something unspoken.

I kept staring at the note, my fingers tracing the ink, my brain wasn't braining anymore. Who was he? Why did he leave this for me?

I carried the note with me for days, tucked inside my journal, hidden between the pages of the book. I told myself I wouldn't call but deep down I knew better, somethings weren't coincidence somethings were meant to happen and this- this felt like one of them.

The Call

It was late when I finally dialed the number, the city outside was quiet the moon casting silver shadows across my room. The phone rang once, twice and then- he answered

"I was wondering when you'd call." his voice was smooth like he had been expecting this.

"I thought of not calling you", I said.

"But you did!"

"Who are you?" I finally asked. A pause and then the answer changed everything.

"Someone you have met before; someone you have forgotten." he said.

"I barely remembered anything from the past" but something about his voice made me doubt myself so after the call ended, I rushed to my bookshelf pulling out an old journal from my childhood. I flipped through the pages, scanning the messy handwriting, the doodles, the memories I had forgotten and then- I found it- our picture and his name, Ishaan Shukla written repeatedly, he was my Neighbour and my friend I had once known. My hands trembled as I traced the ink. He was telling the truth; I had met him before and now- we were finding our way back to each other.

Ishaan's name was written all over my childhood journal, our picture was the proof that he had been a part of my life. Proof that I had once knew him, so why – why had I forgotten him?

I spent days trying to piece it together, flipping through old notebooks searching through childhood memories. Something had erased him from my memory something had made me forget, and then- I found the answer.

It was buried in the back of my journal, written in shaky handwriting. "Ishaan is leaving, I don't want to say goodbye I wish I could forget how sad this feels." and then- nothing. No more mentions of him, no more memories just silence, just absence.

I had forgotten him because I wanted to because losing him had hurt too much. And now- he was back, back in my life back in my memories and back in a way that felt like fate. I had spent days piecing together the memories, flipping through old journal tracing the ink of his name written repeatedly, and now- I knew the truth. I called him, this time I didn't hesitate.

"I remember now", I said the moment he picked up.

Then- (a quiet inhale)

"You do?", his voice was deep, smooth but this time there was something else in it- (relief)

"Yes, I found it in my old journal, I saw our picture, I read what I wrote when you left."

(Another pause)

Then- a soft chuckle

"I was wondering you'd remember, Aisha."

After that night, we started talking every day. At first it was just catching up- where life had taken us, what had changed, what had stayed the same but soon, it became more than that- late night conversations, inside jokes, stories about childhood that made us laugh, made us feel like we have never really lost each other. Ishaan was three years older than me but somehow, it didn't feel like a gap.

CHAPTER SEVEN

FATE

I never believed in fate but when I pulled out my childhood journal, everything shifts. It felt like we had always been meant to find our way back to each other and maybe- this time, we wouldn't lose each other again. This was like a shattered reunion after years apart, we finally reunite.

We started talking every day. At first it was just like old times- laughing, teasing, slipping into friendship that felt as easy as breathing, but as our bond grew stronger, I started finding small changes in my behavior- heart racing when he gets too close, a sudden hesitation in my words, the way I catch myself too much about his opinion, I also started noticing things about Ishaan I never did before- how his voice had deepened, the way his laugh lingered in the air, the quiet intensity in his gaze when he listened. Little by little, feelings began to bloom in places they hadn't before.

The moment I didn't expect!

I never thought I'd feel this way. Something was changing- quietly, slowly, like ink seeping into the paper, unnoticed at first but impossible to ignore. It wasn't just friendship anymore. Every interaction seemed special, and yet the questions kept pinning in my head-

"Was this love, how would I know if I was in love."

"Was nostalgia playing trick on me, making everything feel more intense than it really was? Or was this something real?"

Ishaan stood beside me, unaware of chaos inside my mind. We had been talking about nothing when his phone buzzed, a name appeared on the screen, Sarah. He smiled slightly responding quickly without hesitation. Just like that- uneasiness crept in again- sharp and unexpected. I turned away watching the sunset, its colors shifting and bleeding together like the thoughts inside my head.

"You, okay?", asked Ishaan breaking the silence.

"The sunset looks beautiful at this time" I replied instead, hoping to distract him. But he didn't fall for it, he knew me too well

"Aisha!" his voice was quieter now, but firm. I sighed, finally turning to him letting him see the mix of emotions I couldn't understand.

"I can't lie to you... I don't know if I'm okay!"

His brows lifted slightly, curiosity flickering behind his gaze.

"Is it about Sarah?"

I groaned, "why do you notice everything, it's frustrating."

He laughed, stepping closer, watching me carefully "so what is it? jealousy? Worry? Or...something bigger?"

I folded my arm, pretending to be annoyed, "do you want me to say it?"

"I mean I won't stop you" he teased

I rolled my eyes, "you love making things dramatic, don't you?"

He laughed, shaking his head "I think you do too!"

And maybe he was right maybe I liked the way he danced around feelings, teasing and testing the boundaries of whatever this was, maybe I liked how he understood me without me saying a word.

Then, I watched as Ishaan set up his canvas, his movements so calm. He had always loved to paint- not just for the sake of art but because it was the way he saw the world, the way he captured emotions without saying a single word, the sun was melting into the horizon its colors shifting between shades of amber and violet, and Ishaan completely lost in his craft began to paint. I stood there watching him. Watching the way his fingers moved with certainty, the way he paused for few moments, tilting his head, thinking and feeling. He didn't rush, he never rushed, he saw things in a way most people didn't. He appreciated every detail, gave time to everything- whether it was a painting, a conversation or a person. And that's when it hit me. Not in some dramatic way, NO! it was quiet, it was simple, it was the slow realization that had been creeping into my mind all this time, spreading through me like ink into paper. This was the person, the one I wanted beside me in every sunset, in every moment, in every chapter of my life.

I had been so caught up in figuring out what love was, so tangled in questions and uncertainties, that I hadn't realized I already had the answer.

Ishaan turning slightly, glancing at me "what?" he asked, chuckling "you're staring!"

"Nothing, you looked so lost in it like the world didn't exist outside of this canvas." I shake my head at my own inability to find the right words.

He had all the qualities I'd like in a partner, from the moment he walked into my life, he became the center of my universe, the source of my joy and reason for my smile, with each passing day my love for him started growing deeper and stronger, yes! I fall in love with him, but admitting it? that was the hardest part, because I was worried that news feelings might ruin our friendship.

Something deep I realized

Have you ever heard a song couple of times and thought "Damn this is the best song I've ever heard."

At first, it's just another time playing in the background. Youve heard it before, but it never really stood out. Then one day, something changes. The beat feels stronger; the lyrics speak to you and suddenly its different. It's no longer just a song- it's the song, the one you want to hear repeatedly. The one that stays in your mind long after the music stops. You start noticing every word, every note, every little detail that makes it special. You can't get enough of it.

Falling in love with the person is the same. At first, they are just another person in your world – someone familiar, someone you've seen before, maybe you've talked a few times, maybe you know their name. But one day something about them standout, maybe it's the way they laugh, the way their eyes sparkle or how they say your name in a way that feels different. Suddenly, you want to talk to them more. One conversation turns into many.

You start thinking about them even when they aren't around. You notice the small things- the way they move, the warmth in their voice, the way they look at you. Before you realize it, you're completely drawn in. They are in your thoughts, in your heart, in every quiet moment. They are like your favorite song- the one you keep playing and never get tired, so you press repeat again and again and again, so I think falling in love is like discovering your favorite song.

Unspoken until now

I could hear my heartbeat- fast, loud, restless.

The letter felt heavier in my hands than it should. I had rehearsed this a hundred times in my head and yet sitting across from Ishaan everything I had planned scattered like autumn leaves in the wind. Thoughts kept whirling- "Would this change everything?", "What if it ruined us?" but I couldn't keep it inside anymore

"Ishaan", I said my voice barely above a whisper.

He turned to me; his eyes filled with familiar warmth- the same warmth that had made me fall for him in the first place. I swallowed the lump in my throat and handed him the letter. I watched as he unfolded it, his fingers carefully smoothening the creases, the way he always did when handling something precious. His eyes darted across the words that I had poured my heart into, every letter an echo of love I had kept hidden for so long. I wanted to look away, but I couldn't and then he laughed, not the kind of laugh that mocked, not the kind that brushed things aside – no, this was different. His eyes scanned the words,

"I still remember the first time seeing you after ten years of being apart, I still remember how I fell in love with you and your smile and how everything happened unexpectedly. I'm beyond blessed and thankful that someone like you came into my life, thankyou- thank you for making me feel happy. I accept you for who you are, I want you to know that I truly love you Ishuu, I know it is a little cringe, but it is what it is!"

By the time he finished reading, "Do you know?" he murmured, folding the letter carefully, looking at me with a gaze that felt different- deeper.

"I asked you once, how would I know if was in love?" he let out a small chuckle, shaking his head.

"You were right- I dint need anyone to tell me, I already knew." I blinked, not trusting my voice, not trusting the emotions swirling inside like a storm. Then, his fingers brushed against mine, a simple touch, but one that sent a rush of warmth through me and then- he held my hand.

"I love you too, Aisha." he said, his voice steady as if he had always known. I laughed- half a sob, half disbelief and just like that, every fear, every hesitation melted away, because somehow against all odd, he had fallen for me too.

The promise

I still don't know how I managed to confess. The letter was supposed to stay hidden in my bag folded neatly tucked away like my feeling had been. But something inside me had pushed forward, made me speak, made me hand over those words to Ishaan. And now? Now everything was different- but in the best way possible. Since the moment, Ishaan has been warmer, closer. We don't hesitate to hold hands anymore; there is a quiet understanding between us.

But today- today, he does something unexpected. We're sitting on the rooftop, the city stretched out beneath us. The wind is cool, carrying the scent of monsoon rains, and Ishaan is staring at me, then before I could ask what's wrong, he pulls out a folded piece of paper.

"I have something for you." he says

I hesitate, "what's this?"

His lips twitch, "A response!"

I blink, my fingers shake as I take paper from him, slowly unfolding it. The moment my eyes land on the words, my heart stops.

"Aisha, I don't know the right words to say- so I hope these are enough. I remember that day we met again after years apart, you walked in smiling, like time hadn't taken you away from me. But something had shifted- I had shifted. I didn't realize then, but I was already falling and now here are we. You are braver than me, putting everything into words, before I could. You are my favorite person, my home, my everything and I hope u know- I choose you! Always."

I read it once, twice, thrice times. I blink rapidly, trying to push away the tears threatening to spill.

"Ishaan..." I whisper, looking at him trying to find words. But he just smiles, not his usual, teasing one- no, this one is deeper and softer.

"You don't need to say anything" he murmurs "I just wanted you to know, Aisha."

A breathless laugh escapes me, mixed with disbelief and overwhelming emotions. I reach out, gripping his hand tightly, as if to confirm he's real, that those words aren't just something I imagined. He squeezes my fingers in return, I know this isn't just confession, this is a promise.

When love turns to silence

A few months passed and I started going to college.

Ishaan wasn't the same. I noticed it in the small things first- the way his replies got shorter, how he stopped waiting for me after class like he used to. At first, I convinced myself he was busy, just tired. I told myself that maybe this was just a phase, that he would come back to me like always. But deep down, I knew something was different, something had shifted.

I tried; God I tried. Even when my own life got hectic, when eleventh grade pulled me in different directions, I always carved out time for him, always made sure he was still my safe place, but he didn't meet me halfway, excuses piled up. Texts became unread, conversations felt forced and then one day, no last hug, no last words, no closure

He just.... gone, leaving me shattered! How do you process heartbreak when you don't even get an ending? I kept replaying everything in my head, wondering where I went wrong, what I could have done differently to make him stay. And then I found out the truth, he had fallen for someone else, someone more attractive, more pretty.

While I was breaking myself trying to hold onto him, he had already moved on- already replaced me or maybe that was the reason he left me.

Every moment we shared, every word he had ever said, every promise whispered under city lights.... all of it? Fake. I kept asking myself- was any of it real? Did he ever truly love me, had every word he spoken been rehearsed? had every moment we shared just been a lie?

The pain of betrayal is different from the pain of heartbreak. I didn't deserve this at all. I deserved honesty, I deserved respect, I deserved a love that wouldn't walk away the moment something new caught attention.

I knew one thing for certain- this pain wouldn't define me. One day I would heal, one day I would wake up and realize that losing Ishaan was not my loss, it was his. Because while I had loved him with everything I had, he had chosen to throw that away. And that? That was his mistake.

CHAPTER EIGHT

FROM LOVE TO ASHES

A poetry capturing the beauty of love that eventually burned down into betrayal.

We were just friends
So young, so free
No thoughts of love, no thoughts of we
The years passed by; we lost our way...
Till fate returned one fateful day
Fate called and he was drawn
A book, a note, a spark so bright
A name once lost, brought to light...
Day by day, he held me close
Made me feel like I mattered the most
I loved him true, with all my soul
But love was never his true goal...
For beauty called and he obeyed
Chased another, left me betrayed
His love was false, his words were lies
Left me drowning in silent cries...
Now I stand with lesson learnt
A page once filled, a chapter turned

I won't look back, I won't pretend
Love is not a road I will walk again
I loved, I lost, I learnt to see
That love was never meant for me...
No more chasing, no more pain
I walk alone and feel no shame...
That's my story, the love is done
No more chasing, no place to run
No more waiting, no more pain
No more losing in loves cruel game......

CHAPTER NINE

DROWNING IN DISTRACTIONS

I never imagined my life would take such a sharp turn. Ishaan and I were inseparable—we were two souls bound together by promises, dreams, and unwavering love. Or at least, I thought it was love. The day he betrayed me was the day I felt the ground disappear beneath my feet. He left me for someone else. Someone he found more beautiful, more attractive.

As if love was something so shallow, so easy to discard. For over a year and a half, we had built something together—memories, laughter, plans. And yet, he walked away like it meant nothing. The worst part? He hadn't told me the truth when I confessed my feelings to him.

Back then, he accepted me with open arms, made me believe I was his world. And now? Now I was just another chapter he chose to rip out and throw away.

At first, I thought of erasing him from my life forever. Deleting every message, tearing apart every picture, silencing the echoes of his laughter in my mind. But no matter how hard I tried, his betrayal clung to me like a shadow. The bitterness refused to fade, making its way into my thoughts, my heart, my very existence.

And then came my 12th board exams. The timing couldn't have been worse. The weight of heartbreak pressed down on me, clouding my mind, distracting me from everything else. I studied I studied harder than I ever had—but my heart wasn't in it.

I managed to pass, though barely, stumbling across the finish line with exhaustion rather than triumph. But that wasn't the end. Something even more difficult loomed ahead—NEET, the National Eligibility cum Entrance Test. The biggest test of my life, the key to my dreams, the gateway to everything I had ever worked for. But my mind was elsewhere. My heart was shattered, my focus was lost, and no matter how much I tried, I couldn't silence the storm raging inside me.

When the results came, the truth hit me harder than I expected—I hadn't scored well enough to get admission into any college. The realization crushed me. It felt like I had failed myself. Not just in love, but in life too.

But then I knew—I couldn't let this define me.

I couldn't let one person's betrayal ruin my future. Ishaan might have walked away, but I was still here, and I was stronger than he ever thought I could be.

So, I decided. I would take a drop. I would dedicate myself entirely to my studies, remove every distraction, every doubt. I would give NEET one more shot, but this time, with all my heart and soul. I refused to let my pain become my weakness; instead, I would turn it into my greatest strength. Because in the end, I realized something important—Ishaan's loss wasn't mine. He lost someone who truly loved him, someone who gave everything without hesitation. But I? I was about to find myself.

And this time, no one could take that away from me.

The heartbreak beyond love

I had done everything right this time. I cut out every distraction, locked myself away with my books, and poured every ounce of my soul into my studies. I refused to let the past define me. Ishaan's betrayal had hurt, but I had used that pain to fuel me. I had turned my heartbreak into motivation, shaping myself into someone stronger, someone determined, someone who wouldn't let failure touch me again. But then—fate had its own cruel plans

I thought heartbreak was the worst thing life could throw at me. I thought betrayal was the deepest wound I'd ever feel. I thought failing once was enough pain for a lifetime.

I was wrong.

This time, it wasn't just loss—it was death.

Just months before my second attempt at NEET, when my dreams felt so close I could almost touch them, fate decided I hadn't suffered enough.

It took her.

My coach, my mentor, my guide—the one person who had believed in me when I couldn't believe in myself. She was my strength, my anchor through every storm, my light in the darkest nights of doubt. And then, she was gone. Just like that. A sudden stop of blood flow. A cruel twist of fate that didn't warn me, didn't prepare me, didn't give me time to say goodbye.

Yesterday, she had spoken to me about my exam strategy. Yesterday, she had given me advice with the same warmth and encouragement she always had. Yesterday, I had leaned on her strength, believing she would be there until the very end of this battle.

Today, she was just a memory.

It didn't feel real. It felt like a nightmare I would wake up from, like someone had played a cruel joke on me and would soon tell me it wasn't true. But it was true. It was terrifyingly, painfully true.

I broke.

I cried like I had never cried before. It wasn't just sadness—it was agony, raw and unfiltered. A kind of pain that made breathing feel impossible; a kind of grief that made me forget how to function.

I called Ryaan, my best friend, sobbing so violently I could barely form words. He listened. He consoled me. He told me everything would be okay.

But it wouldn't.

Nothing could bring her back. Nothing could undo the fact that someone who meant everything to me had been ripped away from this world.

And when NEET arrived, my hands trembled as I held my pen. My mind was blank. My heart felt too heavy for me to carry. I had prepared, I had fought, I had sworn I would make this attempt my victory—but none of it mattered anymore.

I failed again.

This failure wasn't like the last. This time, I hadn't just lost a dream. I had lost a person.

Grief became my new companion. Sleepless nights stretched endlessly. I spent hours staring at the ceiling, wondering how the world could keep moving while mine had come to a halt.

I was lost. Completely, devastatingly lost.

But somewhere, in the depths of that unbearable sorrow, a voice whispered a promise I had made long before heartbreak, long before death.

I wanted to be a doctor.

And what did doctors do? They saved lives. They fought against the very thing that had stolen her from me.

So, I couldn't stop. I wouldn't stop.

Through pain, through loss, through an agony that felt eternal—I would rise again.

I took another drop. Another year. Another fight.

Because this time, I wasn't just chasing a dream. I was chasing justice for those who never got another chance.

Nothing's going to stop me now!

Failure.

The word had haunted me for two long, painful years. It followed me like a shadow, lurking in every quiet moment, whispering in the back of my mind when I dared to dream. It had become a part of me— a wound I carried, a weight I bore.

Twice, I had tried. Twice, I had poured my heart into my studies. Twice, life had cruelly knocked me down, each time harder than before.

But I refused to surrender.

Because surrender meant accepting that every tear I had shed, every sleepless night spent battling self-doubt—had been for nothing. And that? That wasn't an option.

This time, there would be no distractions.

No social media. No idle conversations. No excuses.

This was my final fight, and I was prepared to give it everything I had.

And it was brutal.

I spent months locked in battle with my own thoughts, waging war against doubt and exhaustion.

I woke up before the sunrise every day, books spread across my desk, pages filled with calculations, notes scattered across my bed like battle plans.

There were moments when I felt the world closing in. Moments when fear gripped my throat, when frustration pushed me to the edge. Had I made the right choice? Was I setting myself up for another fall? Was I chasing an impossible dream?

Every time doubt crept in, I fought back.

I remembered my teacher—her belief in me, her endless encouragement, the way she had always pushed me forward when I felt lost. I remembered my parents—their sacrifices, their silent prayers, the hope in their eyes every time they told me, "We know you can do this." I remembered Ryaan—my best friend, the one who had never let me drown in despair, who had always reminded me that failing didn't mean I was a failure.

And most importantly, I remembered myself—the girl who had once let heartbreak shatter her, who had faced grief and pain and setbacks but still chose to rise.

The night before the results, I couldn't sleep.

I prayed, I paced, I held my breath as I stared at the ceiling, begging the universe, fate, destiny— anything to let me have this moment.

And then, the morning came.

The results were out.

All India Rank: 47.

For a moment, I stopped breathing.

It was unreal.

Had I read it correctly? Was this real? Was I dreaming?

I checked again. And again. And again.

And then—I cried.

Not soft, quiet tears. These were the kind of tears that erupted like a storm, the kind that carried the weight of years of struggle, years of doubt, years of holding onto hope when hope felt impossible.

My parents ran to me, pulling me into their arms, holding me so tightly I thought I might break, but I didn't care. Their voices shook with happiness, their pride shining through their teary eyes.

The first person I called? Ryaan.

He screamed into the phone. He laughed, he cried, he called me "unstoppable" and told me he never had a single doubt that I would do it.

We celebrated. We laughed. We let the joy spill over like sunlight breaking through the storm.

I had won.

I had defied heartbreak, grief, doubt, failure, and proven to myself that I was capable of greatness.

And yet through all the celebration, through all the joy, one thought refused to leave my mind.

My teacher.

She should have been here.

She should have been the first person I called.

She should have seen me live up to every belief she had in me.

I wished more than anything, that I could hear her voice one last time, hear her tell me she was proud.

But somewhere, in the depths of my heart, I knew—she had seen.

This victory was not just mine.

It was hers, my parents, Ryaan's and everyone who stood by me through the storm.

And now, as I stepped forward into my future, I knew that no matter what life threw at me next.

I would never break again.

I had risen from the ashes. I had become unstoppable.

A celebration of dreams!

After years of struggle, heartbreak, and relentless perseverance, I had passed NEET—and not just passed, but with an All-India Rank of 47.

I stared at the screen; my breath caught in my throat. My heart thundered in my chest, drowning out every sound around me.

Was this real?

Had I actually done it?

My fingers trembled as I checked the result again—one more time, just to be sure. But the number didn't change. The rank stood there, clear and undeniable.

I had won.

A sob tore from my lips, my vision blurring with tears. I clapped my hand over my mouth, trying to contain the overwhelming surge of emotions crashing over me like a tidal wave.

Years of pain. Years of sacrifice. Years of pushing past every doubt, every failure, every heartbreak.

And today— it all led to this moment.

I turned, searching for the one person who had carried this dream long before I did.

My mother.

She stood frozen, staring at me, waiting for confirmation that she wasn't just imagining things. And then, the realization hit her—her daughter had achieved the dream she had once chased, the dream she had let go of when life took a different path.

Her lips trembled. A sharp breath escaped her.

And then- she broke.

Tears spilled down her cheeks as she threw her arms around me, holding me so tightly I could feel the weight of every sacrifice she had made for me, every unspoken wish, every silent prayer, every dream she had once buried within herself.

She had once wanted to be a doctor.

But circumstances hadn't been kind.

A rank below lakhs had sealed her fate. The only way forward had been to pay for a seat—something impossible, something beyond reach. So instead, she had taken a different road, becoming a science lecturer, shaping young minds, passing on the knowledge she had once dreamt of using in practice.

And today- her dream had come alive through me.

Her voice cracked as she whispered, "I am so proud of you, Aisha."

The warmth in my chest spread, and suddenly, every sleepless night, every tear, every moment of doubt had been worth it.

I had made her dream a reality.

My father pulled me into his embrace next, his pride shining through his teary eyes. He stroked my hair gently, his voice thick with emotion. "You did it, beta. You really did it."

The moment felt endless, like time had frozen just so we could hold onto it forever.

But there was one person missing- Ryaan.

Though he wasn't physically here, his presence was woven into every second of this victory.

He had gotten into IIT Madras, pursuing his own dreams while I fought for mine. But distance had never severed our bond. We had stayed connected through letters, through calls, through every moment where I felt like giving up.

So, as soon as I could breathe again, I grabbed my phone, dialing his number with shaking fingers.

The call barely rang before he picked up, his voice breathless, as if he already knew what I was about to say.

I tried to speak.

Tried to form words.

But all that came out was a shaky, broken sob— "I did it, Ryaan."

And he screamed.

"YOU DID IT, AISHA! OH MY GOD, YOU DID IT!"

His laughter was raw and loud, filled with every ounce of unwavering belief he had always had in me.

We laughed, we cried, we celebrated together, despite the miles between us.

Because this victory? It wasn't just mine.

It belonged to my mother, my father, my teacher who had believed in me, and Ryaan, who had never let me sink into despair.

It belonged to every sacrifice, every tear, every silent hope that had led me here.

And as I stood there, surrounded by the people who meant everything to me, I knew—

This wasn't just an achievement.

This was the beginning of something greater.

CHAPTER TEN

A NEW WORLD

2030,
July 3rd
Delhi
Dear Ryaan Mehra,
I am happy that you have got into IIT- Madras and I have got into AIIMS- Delhi but it feels strange to not have you here. Delhi is different, AIIMS is challenging, harder than I ever imagined. I miss our festivals, the laughter we shared and simplicity of our school days. Tell me all about your classes, campus and the friends you've made. I can't wait to hear all this. You have always inspired me and will still do.
Take care,
Aisha.

2030,
July 6th
Madras
Dearest Aisha,

Life at IIT madras is great. But I really miss you a lot and our festivals too, I miss seeing you light up when you talked about your dreams and plans and yes life feels serious now, but I guess that's what happens when you start chasing big dreams. I have made few good friends here but no one quite like you, you're incredible Aisha, and you've always been. Take care bestie!

Yours,
Ryaan Mehra.

First and second year of MBBS

The transition from my hometown to AIIMS Delhi felt like being thrown into an ocean with no shore in sight.

There was excitement, yes but also an overwhelming sense of uncertainty, pressure, and sheer exhaustion.

MBBS was not just difficult—it was relentless.

It felt like running a marathon with no finish line, a constant cycle of lectures, practical, assignments, and exams that never seemed to stop. The nights stretched endlessly, filled with anatomy diagrams scattered across my desk, pages of dense medical textbooks, and cups of coffee that barely kept me awake.

And in the middle of it all, I felt like a small fish lost in a vast ocean.

But slowly, I began to adapt.

Friendships became my anchor, pulling me through the chaos, reminding me that even in the hardest moments, I wasn't alone.

One of the people who stood by me was Mansi—a tall, stylish girl with a striking wolf cut that made her presence impossible to ignore.

She was bold, confident, effortlessly attractive—but beyond all that, she was optimistic in a way I desperately needed. While I drowned in stress, she taught me to find joy in small victories—a high score on a test, a rare evening free from studying, a cup of chai shared between practical.

Her laughter, her energy—it made the burden feel lighter.

Late-night study sessions became our routine, hours spent buried in textbooks, whispering late into the night about dreams, frustrations, and the quiet longing for home.

Because no matter how much we tried to settle in, Delhi wasn't home. The ache of missing home crept in when I least expected it. The absence of familiar streets, family dinners, and childhood comforts weighed heavy on my chest.

But I had dreams to chase. And I wasn't alone. Among the people I grew closer to was Atharva.

A tall guy with ombre hair that blended into pale skin, his transparent glasses resting perfectly on his sharp features. Handsome? Yes. But beyond looks, he had a way of making everything feel lighter, even on the most grueling days.

We shared an unspoken understanding—the silent resilience of two people fighting their own battles but finding strength in companionship.

He and Mansi had been friends long before AIIMS. They had studied their 11th and 12th together, their bond carrying over into college.

Atharva was thoughtful, kind, incredibly supportive—the kind of person who showed up with coffee when I was buried under mountains of textbooks, who somehow knew exactly what to say when frustration threatened to break me.

He had a way of turning even the darkest nights into something bearable, his quiet encouragement pushing me forward when I doubted myself.

Between cadaver dissections, medical exams, and the never-ending cycle of studying, these friendships became my strength.

They reminded me that MBBS wasn't just about survival, It was about finding the people who made the journey worth it.

Unspoken feelings

Over time, my bond with Mansi and Atharva grew stronger.

They weren't just friends anymore—they had become my safe space, my constants, my family away from home.

But while Mansi and I laughed freely, teasing each other over cups of chai and late-night study sessions, there was something different about Atharva.

With him, there was always a quiet weight in the air—an unsaid truth, a lingering emotion that he never voiced.

And somewhere deep down, I knew what it was.

Atharva's feelings for me had grown over time, shifting from quiet admiration into something deeper, something delicate, something dangerous.

For Atharva, I was light—the person who made his world brighter, the presence that turned exhausting days into bearable ones.

But being close to me wasn't just a blessing.

It was also a challenge, a battle, a bittersweet pain.

Because he loved me.

And yet, he chose to express it in the most silent ways possible—through gestures rather than words, through presence rather than confessions.

When I was drowning in textbooks, he would show up with coffee without me asking. When exhaustion took over, his jokes softened the weight of the day. When frustration made me want to scream, he simply sat beside me, not speaking, just letting me know he was there.

It was love without expectation, without demands, without labels.

But Atharva knew the truth.

He knew that if he confessed, he risked losing what we had.

And so, he hesitated.

He feared that saying the words out loud would ruin everything—just like I had once feared before confessing my feelings to Ishaan. He didn't want to gamble the bond we had, the closeness we shared.

The confession

By the time we reached our second year at AIIMS, Atharva could no longer hold his feelings back.

I had seen the way he looked at me—the quiet longing, the hesitation in his words, the way he showed up for me even when he himself was breaking inside.

And yet, I had tried to ignore it.

Tried to pretend that our friendship was untouched by emotions deeper than companionship.

But that night—under the dim glow of the hospital garden lights, surrounded by the quiet hum of the city beyond the gates—he finally spoke.

His voice trembled, barely above a whisper, but I felt the weight of his words even before he finished them.

"Aisha... there's something I need to tell you."

I turned to him, my heartbeat uneven, sensing the storm before it arrived.

"You mean more than just a friend to me. I care about you deeply... I've felt this way for a long time."

The world blurred.

I sucked in a breath, searching for words, searching for anything to make this moment less painful.

I cared about him.

Deeply.

But not in the way he wanted.

I had walked this road before- falling in love, believing in promises, tasting heartbreak and betrayal.

And I never wanted to go through it again.

So, with tears brimming in my eyes, my voice barely steady, I reached for honesty, even when I knew it would hurt.

"Atharva, you have been an amazing friend to me, and I'm so grateful for everything you've done. But because of my past... I can't. I won't walk this road again. I need to heal. I need to focus on myself."

Silence.

Atharva nodded slowly, forcing a smile despite the ache in his chest.

"I understand," he said, but the crack in his voice betrayed the truth. "I just needed you to know how I feel."

He meant it.

But it didn't stop the pain.

The distance that broke us

After Atharva's confession, our friendship began to change.

He started distancing himself, spending more time alone, burying himself in studies.

He respected my feelings, but the distance hurt us both.

I missed the comfort of his presence, the effortless way he had always brightened my darkest days.

But Atharva was struggling.

He turned toward unhealthy habits, isolating himself from friends, avoiding conversations about how he truly felt.

He was stuck, unable to move forward, yet unable to let go.

And I noticed.

I noticed the way he stopped making late-night jokes, how his laughter didn't reach his eyes anymore, how his shoulders sagged beneath the invisible weight of heartbreak.

One sleepless night, I sat in my room, staring at the ceiling, wondering if life would've been easier if Atharva had understood me like Ryaan did—without falling in love. But my bond with Atharva was different. And now, it was layered with pain and unspoken emotions.

A love that asked for nothing

The rain had been falling for hours—soft, steady, relentless.

I wasn't sure why I chose that afternoon to reach out to him.

Maybe because I had spent too many sleepless nights missing his presence, too many moments wondering if things would ever feel the same again.

Maybe because I had realized—losing Atharva as a friend hurt more than rejecting him as a lover.

So, I found him in the campus library, sitting alone, surrounded by books that hadn't been touched in hours.

His fingers rested on an open page, but his eyes weren't really reading—they were lost, unfocused, drowning in a storm only he could see.

I pulled the chair beside him slowly, hesitating before I whispered his name.

"Atharva."

He looked up, and for the first time in weeks, our eyes met.

The exhaustion was visible on his face, dark circles under his eyes, tension in his shoulders. He looked like someone who had spent too long pretending he was okay.

I swallowed hard.

"I'm sorry."

The words felt heavier than I expected, pressing into my chest like a quiet confession.

"I never meant to hurt you. You have been so important to me, and I hate that things have become this way."

For a long second, he didn't say anything.

Then, he sighed—a deep, quiet breath filled with everything he hadn't said.

"I'm sorry too, Aisha."

His voice cracked, just slightly, just enough for me to hear the raw honesty in it.

"I've been holding onto feelings that I knew would only cause pain—for both of us. I just... didn't know how to let go."

And there it was.

The truth neither of us wanted to say, but both of us already knew.

I reached for his hand, not as someone who could love him the way he wanted, but as someone who refused to let him drown in heartbreak alone.

"It's okay. I understand."

In that moment, we knew—our bond would never be the same again. But somehow, we found a way to rebuild.

The Lessons Love Leaves Behind

Love isn't always about having your feelings returned.

Sometimes, love is selfless- choosing someone's happiness over your own desires, even when love isn't reciprocated.

Atharva cared deeply for me.

And despite his love being unfulfilled, he proved that real love is an act of kindness, not possession.

He faced heartbreak, rejection, and loss, but through his pain, he learned growth, self-reflection, and emotional resilience.

It hurt.

It always hurts when love has nowhere to go.

But love that asks for nothing in return is sometimes the purest form of love.

And through that pain, we both learned something.

Letting go isn't easy.

But sometimes, it's necessary to move forward.

Even after the ache lingered, even after the silence settled between us like an unspoken memory, we found a way to rebuild our friendship.

It wasn't perfect.

It wasn't the same.

But it was still real.

And sometimes, that's enough.

This journey teaches us that life is full of emotional highs and lows—and it's how we navigate these moments that shape us into who we are meant to become.

The weight of healing others

The remaining years of MBBS were a storm I didn't know how to navigate.

I carried an invisible burden, one that no one else could see, one that I rarely spoke of.

Grief had stayed with me long after I lost my beloved teacher during my NEET journey.

It haunted me in the quiet moments.

Sometimes, just the sound of the lecture hall, the rustling of notes, the steady voice of a professor explaining diseases was enough to trigger memories I wasn't ready to face.

Memories of betrayal, of heartbreak, of loss that had never fully healed.

Despite my best efforts, I was lost in my thoughts-trapped somewhere between my past and my future, unable to celebrate my victories, unable to feel the joy of what I had achieved.

By the time my second year came to an end, the pressure only increased.

I wrote endless exams, drowning in the cycle of preparation, performance, and exhaustion.

And then came patient case studies.

A whole new layer of complexity, a whole new form of stress, one that took medicine from books to reality.

These weren't just words written in a textbook anymore. These were real people, real illnesses, real lives placed in our hands to diagnose and understand.

And yet, despite the chaos, despite the long hours spent moving between wards and classrooms, I often found myself staring at the ceiling at night, questioning my ability to move forward.

The pressure was crushing.

The expectations were suffocating.

And somewhere in between it all, I started to feel like a stranger in my own body.

I was a medical student, studying how to heal others.

Yet I felt completely broken myself. Medicine teaches you how to understand pain, disease, and recovery.

But what it doesn't teach you, what no textbook will ever tell you—is how to heal yourself when the weight of grief feels impossible to carry.

It doesn't teach you how to face the ghosts of your past while preparing to save lives.

It doesn't teach you what to do when exhaustion turns into emptiness, when success feels hollow, when victories feel like they don't belong to you anymore.

It doesn't teach you how to keep moving forward when every step feels heavier than the last.

But somehow, despite everything - I kept going.

Even when I felt like I was falling apart. Even when I wasn't sure who I was anymore.

Because somewhere deep inside me, I knew healing takes time. Moving forward takes strength. And even the greatest doctors have wounds that take a lifetime to heal.

A Heartfelt Goodbye!

It was during one of my third-year rotations in the oncology ward that I met Riya.

A vibrant young woman in her late twenties, Riya was fighting an aggressive form of cancer, yet she carried herself with grace, optimism, and an infectious laughter that echoed through the halls.

Her presence had a way of filling the room with warmth, making even the bleakest days feel lighter.

She wasn't just a patient—she was a storyteller, an artist of life, painting her world with laughter and resilience.

From the moment we first spoke, I felt an immediate connection with her.

I admired her strength.

I wondered how, despite everything—she managed to remain so hopeful, so strong in the face of such adversity.

In between medical rounds and patient charts, we talked about everything—dreams, memories, the simple joys of life.

For her, every small moment mattered.

She found happiness in watching the sunset from her hospital window, in sharing stories that made her laugh until tears rolled down her cheeks.

But as the days passed, as her condition worsened, her energy began to fade.

Yet still—she lived.

She loved, she laughed, she held on to every second as if time itself was a gift she refused to take for granted.

One afternoon, as I sat beside her, she reached for my hand.

Her fingers were cold, delicate, but her grip was firm.

She handed me a small envelope.

"Open this after I'm gone," she whispered softly.

My heart clenched at the words, but I nodded, my hands trembling as I tucked the envelope safely into my pocket.

Neither of us spoke about what it meant. But we both knew.

A few weeks later, Riya passed away peacefully, surrounded by her family and medical team.

The loss hit me harder than I had expected.

Even knowing it was inevitable, even understanding that medicine couldn't rewrite fate, I still wasn't prepared to say goodbye.

That evening, as rain drizzled against my window, I finally opened the envelope she had given me.

Inside was a handwritten letter, its edges slightly worn from where her fingers had held it.

Her words, carefully crafted in her unique style, felt like a whisper from beyond.

Dear Aisha,

If you're reading this, it means my time here is up. But please don't be sad. I lived a good life, one that was filled with love, laughter, and people like you. I want you to know that your kindness, your compassion, your heart made my days brighter. You were there for me not just as a medical student, but as a friend and that's something I will cherish forever. Promise me one thing. Never lose that spark that makes you stand out. This journey you're on? It's tough. I know. I've seen it in your eyes, in the way you carry the weight of every patient, in the way you question if you're enough. But you are. You've got something special, Aisha. The world needs more doctors like you—ones who see patients as people, not just as cases, Keep that fire alive. And always remember—you made my life greater.

Love, Riya.

Tears streamed down my face as I read each line, my hands shaking, my heart shattering and healing all at once.

Her words became more than just a farewell.

They became a mantra, a reminder of why I had chosen this path.

Not just to treat illnesses.

Not just to diagnose diseases.

But to make lives better, even in the smallest ways.

Even if only for a moment.

And in that moment, I knew—Riya would stay with me forever, guiding me through the rest of my medical journey.

Too young for so much loss!

By the time I reached my third and fourth years of MBBS, life had become more difficult than I ever imagined.

I was too young to carry this much weight.

Too young to face heartbreak that still lingered like an open wound. Too young to see the deaths of people I loved—my teacher, my friend Riya.

Loss had changed me.

It had reshaped the way I looked at the world, at people, at medicine. Nothing felt the same anymore.

Grief didn't announce itself loudly—it wasn't a storm that crashed through my life in one singular moment.

Instead, it crept in silently, lingering in the corners of my thoughts, showing up in unexpected places.

Sometimes, it was triggered by the mere sound of a lecture hall, the echoes of medical discussions reminding me of my teacher—the one who had guided me, believed in me, and was supposed to see me succeed.

Other times, it was in the quiet of the oncology ward, when I looked at another patient fighting for their life and thought of Riya—the way she laughed, the way she had handed me that envelope with a quiet acceptance I still wasn't ready for.

Despite everything I tried, I was lost in my thoughts.

I wasn't able to celebrate victories.

I wasn't able to enjoy the milestones that once meant everything to me.

By the time my second year ended, the pressure had only increased.

Exams felt endless. Studies felt heavier. Then came patient case studies—another layer of complexity that pushed me further into exhaustion.

These were real people, real illnesses, real suffering—things no book could prepare me for.

I listened to their stories, understood their pain, answered their questions—but deep down, I couldn't escape the suffocating thought that I was just as broken as them.

I had spent years studying how to heal others— Yet I didn't know how to heal myself.

I felt like a stranger in my own body—disconnected, unable to understand what I was truly going through.

I knew I couldn't ignore what was happening inside me.

But I also didn't know how to face it.

Grief has no timeline.

Pain doesn't disappear just because you choose to keep going.

And medicine, for all its knowledge, doesn't teach you how to heal yourself when you're falling apart. I didn't know how to move forward, I didn't know how to make sense of the ache in my chest, the exhaustion that felt deeper than just lack of sleep.

I only knew one thing—

I had to keep going anyway.

Seeking Help

Opening meant breaking the silence, admitting that I was struggling, allowing myself to be vulnerable in a way that felt terrifying.

But it was necessary.

Healing didn't come from ignoring pain, from pretending everything was okay.

Healing came from facing it, from allowing others to help carry the weight when it became too much to bear alone.

Mansi and my friends became my anchors, reminding me that I wasn't alone, that strength wasn't about suffering in silence—it was about knowing when to ask for help.

And slowly, I took my first steps toward healing.

Because even the strongest hearts need care, too. I had spent years studying how to heal others.

But now, for the first time, I was the one who needed help.

It felt like a role reversal, like the universe had placed me on the opposite side of the equation—no longer the student diagnosing cases, but the person carrying wounds that no textbook could explain.

Walking into the psychiatrist's office was one of the hardest things I had ever done.

My pulse was unsteady; my fingers curled tightly into my sleeves as if holding onto something tangible would stop the whirlwind of emotions inside me.

Mansi's words echoed in my mind—

"You have been there for everyone, Aisha. Let someone else be there for you."

And so, I did.

I stepped forward.

For the first time, I allowed myself to be seen—not as the future doctor, not as the strong one, but as someone who was lost, exhausted, and quietly breaking beneath the weight of everything she had carried alone.

BACK TO THE PSYCHIATRIST

Walking into psychiatrist office was one the hardest things I had ever done. The plaque on the door in front of me reads; "dr. Nagma Kapoor".

"Here I'm now" I said.

Dr. Kapoor spent her whole time recording my story,

"Thank you for sharing that with me, Aisha. It takes a lot of courage to open like this; I want you to know that what you're feeling is valid and you don't have to go through this alone."

Dr. Kapoor pauses for a moment before continuing, "I'd like to take some time to review everything you've shared with me and discuss it with the senior doctors, in the meantime I think it would be helpful to involve your patients in the process. Would you be okay with me speaking to them?"

I hesitate because the idea of my parents knowing my struggle will make me feel exposed, but I nod, "it's okay." I say quietly

Dr. Kapoor gives me smile saying, "let me talk to them and then we'll plan the next steps together."

I step out into the waiting hall, watching as my parents are called into the office. I find a seat on cold metallic chair, and I sit down. My thoughts swirl with anxiety-how will my parents react? Will they understand?

After an hour, my parents emerge from the office with mixed expressions of worry and determination.

My mother sits beside me, taking my hand and squeezing it gently, "beta, we are here for you." she says softly.

I felt a lump rise in my throat and tears started flowing. Dr. Kapoor joins us in the waiting hall and suggests a combination of regular therapy sessions and lifestyle changes to help me manage my mental health.

"This will be a journey, Aisha but you've already taken the hardest step by seeking help. Thats something to be proud of." she says smiling.

I nod.

My journey

Therapy had slowly begun to put the pieces of my life back together. I was finding joy in small things again—a good cup of chai, Mansi's laughter, the quiet fulfillment of helping patients during my rotations. The weight I carried felt a little lighter each day. But after a grueling term at AIIMS, I decided to visit home, hoping the break would help me reconnect with my roots.

The moment I stepped into my old room, memories came rushing back—failures, struggles, unbearable grief. The loss of my mentor. The absence of Riya, my patient. The sting of betrayal. It was as though my past pains had settled into the walls, whispering their presence no matter how hard I tried to push them away.

One evening, I felt like a burden to my parents, and the thought surfaced—there was only one way out, that was to take my own life. That idea lingered for days until one night, at around eleven, I climbed to the terrace. The cold air hit me, stealing my breath. The sky stretched above me, stars glistening, indifferent to my turmoil. I stepped onto the edge, looking down. Cars, trees, balconies—I had to pick a spot.

I sat on the ledge, gathering the final moments in my mind. And then, as if the universe refused to let me go, a voice broke through my thoughts.

"Oh Maaya, I really love you. All I'm doing is expressing my feelings for you. Just think about it once."

A male voice, filled with hope.

For a fleeting moment, it sounded like Atharva. I turned, my gaze landing on two figures—Abhi, the young man from my building, and Maaya, the girl who had moved in recently. They were deep in conversation, unaware of my presence. The word "love" echoed in my mind, weaving memories of the people who had cared for me—Atharva, whose love I couldn't return but deeply valued; Mansi, with her unwavering friendship; Ryaan, my first best friend, who never stopped believing in me; Riya, who had taught me to find beauty in life, even in its darkest corners.

I stared at Abhi and Maaya—their words, their connection, it was pulling me away from the edge.

And then, another voice.

"Aisha, what the hell are you doing here?"

It was my father.

Panic. Shock.

I turned, tears spilling freely now. He ran toward me; his face twisted with anguish.

"Why, Aisha?" His voice cracked.

I had never seen my father cry. That night, I did. And it broke something inside me.

Abhi and Maaya quietly moved to the other side of the terrace, giving us space. I stood there, unable to find words for the storm inside me. My father wrapped his arms around me, and for the first time what felt like forever, I felt hope—I mattered.

Later that night, he didn't hesitate—he took me straight to Dr. Kapoor's office. Sitting in the waiting room, shame gnawed at me, but when she called me in, her voice was just as warm, just as steady.

"It's good to see you, Aisha," she said gently. "I know today has been difficult, but I'm glad you're here. Let's talk about it."

And so, I did. I told her everything—the thoughts that consumed me, the moment I climbed the terrace, the voices that distracted me, and my father's tear-streaked face. She listened, her expression calm, unwavering.

When I finished, silence hung in the room for a moment before she spoke.

"Thank you for sharing this with me, Aisha. What you went through is something no one should ever have to face alone. But you did something important today—you stepped back. That means there's still a part of you that wants to fight, that wants to heal."

Dr. Kapoor asked me a series of questions, trying to understand my state of mind better. She gently suggested involving my parents in the conversation. I hesitated, but agreed. I knew their support would be crucial for my recovery.

When they entered the office, she explained everything—the importance of a supportive environment, the patience and love that would help me rebuild.

This was a journey. But with time, with love, with hope—I could come out of it stronger.

A new beginning

Returning to college after the incident was troubling me, and returning to college felt like stepping into a battlefield—a war between the past I was running from and the future I wasn't sure I deserved. The halls that had once felt like home now seemed foreign, layered with memories I wasn't ready to face. I could feel them lurking in the lecture rooms, whispering doubts in the quiet corners of the library, waiting for a moment of weakness to pull me under.

But I had nowhere else to go.

Medicine had always been my anchor, my reason for moving forward. It had once given me joy, purpose. If there was any piece of myself left to salvage, I would find it there.

So, I buried myself in my rotations, immersing myself in the rhythm of diagnoses and treatments, losing myself in the science of healing. And then, on one ordinary day, during my dermatology rotation, Riyaz walked into the clinic.

He was just ten years old, but his small frame carried the weight of battles no child should have to fight. His skin bore patches of discoloration—an uncommon condition, harmless in its medical severity but brutal in its consequences. The world had marked him as different. It had branded him with cruelty, bullied him into isolation, made him believe he was something to hide.

When he entered the clinic, his steps were slow, cautious—as if he expected the walls to reject him too. His mother walked beside him, her grip firm yet gentle on his shoulder, carrying the silent exhaustion of a parent trying to mend wounds she couldn't see.

He sat on the examination table, shoulders hunched, gaze fixed on the floor.

I knelt beside him, voice soft, careful.

"Hi Riyaz, I'm Aisha. Can you tell me how you're feeling today?"

Silence.

His mother sighed, pain woven into her words as she spoke for him. She told me about the bullying, the nights spent crying into his pillow, the way he had slowly faded into a version of himself she barely recognized. He hadn't been to school in weeks. He no longer laughed. No longer talked.

I studied him—not the patches on his skin, not the symptoms or medical jargon—but the boy beneath it all. The child who had lost his place in the world.

"What's your favorite book?" I asked.

His fingers clenched around the hem of his shirt. His lips parted, hesitated.

"What about movies?"

Nothing.

"What did you love doing before all of this?"

Stillness.

And then, a whisper.

"I used to draw."

I latched onto the thread of hope, careful not to pull too hard.

"What did you draw?"

A pause. Then, softer—more hesitant than before—he answered.

"Superheroes."

He spoke about them, the way a dreamer talks about stars—distant, unreachable, yet somehow still there, waiting. He had spent hours sketching them, building worlds where he wasn't Riyaz, the boy they mocked. He was something greater. Someone powerful. Someone unbreakable.

After his examination, I sat with him and his mother, mapping out the treatment plan, detailing steps to manage his condition. But before they left, I reached for something beyond medicine.

I handed Riyaz a notebook.

"This is for you," I said, pressing it into his hands. "Every superhero starts with a story. I think it's time for you to write yours."

He lifted his head.

And this time, he looked at me.

Not with the dullness I had first seen. Not with the sadness carved into his being.

But with something else.

A flicker. A spark. A tiny ember of belief—fragile, but there.

And in that instant, I saw myself in him.

The loneliness. The suffocating isolation. The feeling of being different, of being small in a world that refused to see you. The way pain had swallowed me whole, whispering that I didn't matter.

I thought of Mansi, whose kindness had kept me afloat. Of Atharva, whose loyalty had been silent yet unwavering. Of Riya, who had taught me that even in the darkest moments, there was beauty to be found. Of my father, whose tears had reminded me that I was loved beyond measure.

That day, something inside me shifted.

My pain wasn't my enemy. It was my story.

And stories had the power to heal—not just ourselves, but others too.

Maybe that was why I had survived.

So that no one else had to fight alone.

CHAPTER TWELVE

FROM STRUGGLES TO STETHOSCOPES

Becoming a doctor was supposed to be the moment—the grand triumph, the culmination of years spent fighting battles no one saw, pushing through exhaustion, pain, doubt. It was supposed to be the chapter where I finally stood tall, invincible, untouchable.

But when it happened—when the final exam was passed, when the degree was in my hands, when I officially became Dr. Aisha—the weight of it didn't feel the way I had imagined.

It was heavier.

The world cheered around me. My mother's eyes glistened with unshed tears, her pride radiating from every unspoken word. My father shook my hand, then pulled me into a rare embrace, his voice thick with emotion as he whispered, "You did it, Aisha. You did it."

Ryaan, my best friend—my constant—stood by me, the same unwavering presence he had always been. We laughed, we reminisced, he teased me about the sleepless nights I had spent buried in textbooks, but beneath it all, I knew he was proud.

My friends celebrated, voices overlapping in excitement, in joy, in disbelief that we had actually made it.

Dr. Kapoor, my psychiatrist—the woman who had once sat across from me in silence, waiting for me to speak when I thought I had nothing left to say—smiled with quiet satisfaction.

"I always knew you would get here," she said, warmth in her voice. "You fought for it."

And yet, deep within me, there was something tangled beneath the happiness.

Something raw.

Something that felt unfinished.

Because in the quiet moments—the ones where I was alone, where I stared at my reflection wearing the title I had spent my whole life chasing—I still heard the voices of the past.

I heard Riya's laughter, the way she had once told me to find beauty in life, even in its darkest moments.

I heard the agony in my father's voice the night he had pulled me back from the terrace, the way his tears had shattered something inside me.

I saw the echoes of my grief, the people I had lost, the mistakes I had made, the love I had been given but couldn't return.

And yet—I had made it.

Residency came next, bringing challenges that pushed me to the edge of myself. Long shifts that blurred into one another, patients who carried their own burdens, their own battles. I wasn't just treating skin conditions. I was treating people—people who had been mocked for the way they looked, people whose self-worth had been stripped away because the world refused to see beyond imperfections.

I listened.

I understood.

I offered not just treatments but words, moments, reassurance.

Because I knew what it felt like to be different.

I knew what it felt like to stand on the edge and wonder if you mattered.

And slowly—through every conversation, every smile, every moment spent watching a patient regain hope—I found pieces of myself within them.

Healing them, in some way, healed me.

And so, when the residency ended, when the final day came and I stepped forward not just as a doctor, but as a healer—I knew that the journey hadn't ended.

It had only begun.

My mother's smile was the brightest I had ever seen. My father, usually reserved, cried—just a little, before quickly wiping his tears away with a laugh.

"You were always meant for this," he said.

Ryaan, my best friend, threw an arm over my shoulder, grinning as he reminded me of all the times I had nearly quit, all the nights I had doubted myself.

"You proved yourself wrong," he said simply.

And maybe that was the real victory.

Because for so long, I had thought my pain would break me.

But in the end—it shaped me.

It gave me the strength to stand before the world, to hold out my hands, to heal others the way I had once needed healing myself.

CHAPTER THIRTEEN

BEYOND THE WHITE COAT

I had spent years inside hospital walls, beneath fluorescent lights, drowning in textbooks, late-night shifts, and the relentless pursuit of knowledge. Medicine had demanded everything from me—my strength, my time, my resilience. And I had given it willingly, knowing that healing others was the purest thing I could ever do.

Yet, even as I thrived, something restless stirred within me. A whisper. A quiet calling to something beyond prescriptions and diagnoses.

A world of beauty. Of creativity. Of expression.

Growing up, I had admired fashion—not just as a spectacle but as an art form, a way of telling stories without words. The way fabric draped a person, the way light captured movement, the way confidence could radiate from a single, striking pose.

And after years of suppressing that part of me, I felt ready to embrace it once again.

It started as an experiment.

A few skincare photoshoots, blending my dermatological expertise with the artistry of beauty campaigns. I wanted to show people that confidence wasn't about perfection—it was about authenticity, about owning your story, scars and all.

What I never expected was for the industry to notice.

Suddenly, my dual identity, a doctor and a model—became something people talked about, something that challenged conventions. I wasn't supposed to belong in both worlds. Yet, there I was, walking ramps, standing before cameras, proving that identity could be limitless.

Then, one day, I asked myself the question that would change everything.

What if I went further?

The answer led me to the doors of Miss India—an institution drenched in legacy and expectation. I wasn't just stepping into a competition. I was stepping into a battlefield, one where elegance met discipline, and where every contestant carried a story powerful enough to move a nation.

Balancing dermatology with pageantry was an uphill climb. There were grueling rehearsals, interviews, workouts, press conferences. And still, I had to juggle my patients, my clinic, my medical responsibilities.

But I wasn't a stranger to hard work.

I had fought harder battles—battles within myself, battles against the darkness that once tried to consume me. And so, I pushed forward, unwavering.

I knew why I was here.

Through the platform, I raised my voice for mental health awareness. I spoke of resilience, of healing, of finding beauty in survival. I wanted people to know that scars—whether visible or hidden—were not signs of weakness. They were proof that we endured. That we overcame.

Then, the night arrived.

The final stage. The golden glow of the spotlight. The weight of thousands of dreams pressing into the air.

The world watched as the final announcement was made.

"And your Miss India is... Aisha."

There was a beat of silence.

Then—shock. Gasps. Thunderous applause.

I stood there, the crown placed upon my head, drowning in the enormity of the moment.

A doctor. A healer. A model. A fighter.

I had shattered expectations.

I had redefined what it meant to be limitless.

That night, as I looked into the crowd, I realized something that sent a shiver down my spine.

I had spent years searching for who I was supposed to be.

But maybe I was never meant to choose just one path.

Maybe I was meant to be everything.

A force of nature. A voice for change. A beacon for dreamers who dared to defy labels and embrace every part of themselves.

Because the world will always try to tell us who we should be.

But we are the ones who write our own story.

Limitless dreams!

The stage lights gleamed like stars, illuminating the vast auditorium. Rows upon rows of faces stared back at me—some filled with curiosity, some with admiration, and others with the quiet contemplation of a dream they had once buried deep within themselves.

I stood at the podium, my hands steady, my heart full.

This moment.

This was the moment I had fought for. The moment that was never meant to happen, at least not according to the world that once told me I had to choose—between ambition and happiness, between success and love, between practicality and passion.

But today, as I took a deep breath and prepared to speak, I knew one thing for sure:

Our battles do not break us. They build us.

I leaned forward, voice steady but rich with emotion, carrying the weight of everything I had lived through.

"To every teenager out there, to every dreamer who feels lost, to everyone who has questioned their worth. let me tell you something that no one teaches you in school or college.

You will fall in love. You will experience heartbreak. You will feel lost. You will feel alone. You will question yourself."

I paused, scanning the room. Some faces were still. Some eyes blinked rapidly, as though processing words they had never heard spoken so boldly.

"There will be days when the pain feels unbearable. When the world feels too heavy. When it seems easier to give up than to keep fighting.

But hear me loud and clear—you will rise.

You will heal. You will move forward. And one day, you will look back and realize that everything that tried to break you only made you stronger."

I exhaled, my voice unwavering, my soul stripped bare for them to see.

"I know what it feels like to love someone and not be loved back. I know what it feels like to lose people who once meant the world to you. I know the pain of failure, rejection, and doubting your own worth.

But here's the truth—none of it lasts forever."

A hush had fallen over the room, as if the air itself carried my words like fragile glass, afraid to shatter their meaning.

"If people walk away, let them. If your heart breaks, let it. If your dreams seem out of reach, stretch higher."

I let my gaze drift, catching sight of a girl in the front row. She was clutching the arms of her chair, her fingers tense. She reminded me of myself—years ago, sitting in a crowd, desperately needing to hear that I was enough.

"They told me I couldn't be both a doctor and a model. That I had to choose. That life had limits.

But I refused.

I became a dermatologist, helping people feel beautiful in their own skin. I became a model, redefining beauty beyond society's expectations. And today, I wear the crown of Miss India—not just for myself, but for every girl and boy who has ever been told that they cannot have it all."

A soft murmur spread through the audience. I could hear it—the ripple of realization, of hope.

"You don't have to fit into society's idea of success. Build your own version of it.

Love deeply but never lose yourself for anyone. Dream wildly, but do not let fear stop you. Fail. Learn. Try again."

I let the moment settle. Then, I said what I knew they needed to hear the most.

"To every young person listening to me right now—love is one of the most beautiful experiences you will go through.

Maybe you'll have a crush who never notices you. Maybe you'll fall in love deeply, fully. And maybe... it will break you for a little while.

But here's the secret no one tells you:

Love—whether it stays or fades—always teaches you something.

It teaches you how to dream. It teaches you how to hurt. And most importantly, it teaches you how to heal."

The silence was thick now, charged with something electric—something transformative.

I let it linger before speaking again, softer this time.

"If you love someone and it doesn't work out, it doesn't mean you weren't enough.

It simply means they were part of your journey—not your destination.

Love does not define you. YOU define you.

Your heartbreaks, your failures, your fears—they are only chapters.

But you—you have the power to write the rest of the book."

I could see it now—the girl in the front row, her grip on the chair easing, her shoulders relaxing.

Someone in the back wiped away a single, quiet tear.

"The world does not belong to those who play it safe. It belongs to those who dare to dream beyond limits.

And if I could rise, you can too.

Your future is yours to create.

I am not looking at the future.

I am building it."

The final words left my lips, and for a moment, nothing happened.

Then, the world exploded.

Cheers. Applause. Roars of approval, of belief, of something greater than all of us.

I stepped back, overwhelmed, watching as the energy surged through the room, filling the space with something uncontainable—something magical.

I had not just spoken.

I had moved something inside them.

And that—that was the real victory

Epilogue

FIVE YEARS LATER

The world around Aisha changed and so had she, five years passed since she stood on miss India stage, wearing the crown but her journey had not stopped there, it had only expanded leading her to new dreams and new challenges. Aisha now sat in her dermatology clinic a space she had built with passion, patients came to her not only for treatment but for something deeper- confidence. She understood their insecurities because she had once struggled with her own, she listened she transformed lives, proving that beauty wasn't just about appearance but about embracing one's own uniqueness. Yet, her life was more than medicine, the world of fashion still welcomed her and she graced runways not just in India but across the globe. Paris, Milan, Newyork- the places she once dreamed of were now part of her reality. One day, she glanced down at her phone messages poured in; her family sending their love, Mansi reminding her that she is incredible, Atharva and Ryaan – still her closest friends but one message stood out from someone she never met, " I heard your story- I was lost, but now I know I can rise too. thank you." a soft smile spread across Aisha's lips this was it had always been about- not titles, not magazine covers, not fame, it was about impact.

If she did it maybe you can too!

Author's Note

Okay, let's get one thing straight—this book is fiction, but the energy, the emotions, and the hustle? All 100% real. The names and details might be made up, but the grind, the dreams, and the vibes? Absolutely authentic.

Life is lowkey messy. You think you have it all figured out, and suddenly—boom. Plot twist. But honestly? That's where the magic happens. Success isn't about following some boring script. It's about adapting, thriving, and making moves—even when the world tells you it's impossible.

Now let's talk about ME, a 14-year-old, stepping straight into the 'Doing Big Things' era. Writing a book? Massive flex. Was I scared? Absolutely. Did I doubt myself? More times than I can count. BUT GUESS WHAT? I had THE backbone of my existence—my sister. Juhi, if I'm the main character, YOU are the rock-solid foundation keeping it all together. Every single time I spiraled, overthought, or hit a full existential crisis moment, you were there, hyping me up, dragging me back into reality, and reminding me that I was BUILT FOR THIS.

Then, my parents—Jagdish and Neeta Thakur. The GOATs of unconditional love and dream support. You taught me how to dream loud, work hard, and never settle. You made me believe I could do anything, and honestly? You were right. I love you endlessly.

My twin, Jaidev—bro, you casually dropped a suggestion, and BOOM! here I am, with an ACTUAL BOOK. You're iconic for that. Appreciate you forever.

To my grandparents, your belief in me is the kind of strength that keeps me going—I carry it always.

To my sweetest little brother, Tanish, the most patient person ever—thank you for letting your chaotic Didi disappear into writing mode. You're the best, and I appreciate you SO MUCH.

And to my besties, Sahasra and Jeeshitha —listen, I know you're reading this freaking out. Like, WHAT?! YOU WROTE A BOOK AND DIDN'T TELL US?! Yes. Yes, I did. NGL, keeping this a secret wasn't easy. You two know everything about me—probably more than I know about myself—but somehow, I managed to pull off the ultimate "SURPRISE, BESTIES!!" moment.

And to ALL MY FRIENDS, you already know the vibes. You make life better, funnier, wilder, and more unforgettable. THANK YOU for being part of my story.

Helen Keller once said, "Although the world is full of suffering, it is also full of the overcoming of it." And this book? Proof that even when life throws doubts, challenges, and chaos, WE LEVEL UP, DREAM BIGGER, AND WRITE OUR OWN STORY.

So let this be a reminder to never play small, never hold back, and never let anyone tell you that your dreams are too much, your dream has NO limits.

Jeevika thakur

15th May 2025